NIGHT CRIES

NOCTURNAL SCREAMS: VOL 1

Mark Leslie

PUBLISHING

Stark Publishing
Waterloo, Ontario
www.starkpublishing.ca

NIGHT CRIES: Nocturnal Screams Volume 1 / Mark Leslie
April 2020

For the monster under my bed. Thanks for all the years of inspiration.

Table of Contents

Introduction

IN MY 2004 book *One Hand Screaming*, a collection of macabre stories and poems, I confessed to the fact that I screamed a lot. Silent screams, I called them. Story ideas bouncing around inside my head like an impending storm. I also admitted to being a condemned man; condemned to write. And, in particular, to write tales from just outside the normal realm. Tales that explore the shadows, that relish in the unknown, the eerie.

Not much has changed from then to now.

Sure, I have a decent number of books under my belt, but the silent screams never went away. They merely manifested them in different ways, from explorations of non-fiction true ghost story books to full length horror and thriller novels.

But my passion for short fiction has never wavered.

That's the special joy out of being a writer, a storyteller. Stories, characters, situations, ideas come to you. They never stop coming to you. They never stop intriguing. Some of them take form in short quick tales; others demand longer full-length forms.

I love them all.

But I'm still quite fond of shorter works. There's nothing like being able to enjoy a short story in a single sitting as a reader. And there's also a special pleasure that comes from being able to express the inspiration for a tale in a shorter, self-contained work.

That's one of the reasons why I wanted to return to some of those shorter works and share them in a series of connected collections that follow me as I whistle past the proverbial graveyard.

Collected here are three short stories specifically following a particular theme. They involve the night, or darkness, as well as the things that can hide in those shadows.

One of the stories has never been published before. Another was published in a small press magazine, and yet another was released in a limited-edition chapbook for a Con where I was one of the Guests of Honor. But I think they play off of one another nicely into this volume's particular theme of "Night Cries."

But enough introductory chatter. You're here to enjoy some short fiction. Come, take my hand, let's explore sensory deprivation at its deepest and darkest, the horrors of being able to see things that others never notice and the unexpected eerie delivery of a treat that normally makes a student's mouth water.

Taste of Darkness

DALE JOHNSON WAS immediately enveloped by the darkness. Merely one step into the room, he turned to look at the doorway he had just entered but could not see it. The annoying Muzak which had been playing in the hallway began to fade as well, as if someone was turning down the volume.

Mr. Jacks had been right. It was as if he was no longer inside the newly renovated health club, but instead in some other dimension completely removed from the natural world.

His senses surrendered to the darkness, leaving him first with no sight, then no sound. As he continued to stand there his sense of touch began to dull, as if under a slow-working anesthetic, and he could no longer smell the fresh paint from the hallway.

The only sense which apparently remained was taste.

Mr. Jacks had promised it would be an incredible sensation when the only thing you could experience was the bitter-sweet taste of darkness.

This was perfect. It was an excellent place to meditate on life's problems and decisions. More clearly than he was usually able to, Dale began to think about the promotion he had applied for. The circumstances of his workplace floating calmly through his mind, he felt right about the promotion. He was the most experienced, hardest working employee in the department, able to motivate and train fellow co-workers. There was no way the position of department manager could not be his. And in the back of his mind, the thought that the promotion of the single black man in the department could be construed by his colleagues as "affirmative action" also faded. Any negative spark he might have had about the situation seemed to be smothered in the calming blanket of darkness.

Dale shuddered and stepped toward where the doorway should be. He passed through it and stood in the hallway again, the darkness sliding off him like so much shed skin, revealing the light, the pervading smell of fresh paint and the saccharine sweet sound of Muzak.

Mr. Jacks stepped out from the office across the hall, his bushy eyebrows raised high on his forehead. His lips, pursed, were obscured by his thick moustache. Give him a larger nose and a pair of thick glasses, Dale quickly realized, and you'd think he was wearing one of those novelty shop disguises.

But despite his small stature – almost a full foot shorter than Dale Johnson – and his Groucho Marx features, there was something respectful about him. Dale assumed it was the reservedness with which he spoke.

"Well?" Mr Jacks said.

"This room is perfect," Dale said, feeling a sudden rumbling in his stomach. "It's better than any sensory deprivation tank I've ever been in. How much?"

Mr. Jacks smiled an ugly grin that managed to peek out from under his moustache. "It's already paid for."

"What?"

But there was no response. Mr. Jacks simply turned on the spot and went back into the office. The office door quietly closed behind him and Dale was left with the Muzak and the paint.

And the gentle moan of his stomach.

Sitting in the deserted Jacks Health Club cafeteria, Dale crunched down the tasteless tofu burger, then sipped at the bland orange juice. Either the food was off because this was the first day that the club was open for business or he was coming down with a cold. None of the food he'd had for lunch could curb his appetite or affect his taste buds, never mind please them.

And what was it that Mr. Jacks meant about it already being paid for? He was certain that the sensory deprivation room was not part of his membership fees at the club. It was listed nowhere on the brochures and Mr. Jacks specifically said, before he even began his tour of the facilities, that there would be an extra charge to use any of the areas other than the pool, the showers, the weight room and the exercise machines.

So how, then, could Dale's use of the sensory deprivation room be paid for? Would Mr. Jacks simply add it to the bill and withdraw it out of his account along with the regular monthly membership fee? Probably – but there was something about the way he'd smiled that disturbed Dale.

He finished his lunch, swiped at his face with the napkin and made his way toward the locker room. Mr. Jacks had provided him with a key and a locker number; before he left he might as well have a look at where it was.

On his way to the locker room glanced at a clock on the wall and did a double take.

He looked at his watch. It was a quarter past three.

But that's impossible, he thought.

He had come to this facility at shortly after ten that morning. It had taken him maybe half an hour to tour the facility, perhaps fifteen minutes to order and eat lunch and he'd spent only five or so minutes in the isolation room.

Hadn't he?

Perhaps he'd stayed in the isolation room longer than he was aware. It sometimes happened. And it would account for the intense hunger he'd felt – after all, he'd skipped breakfast and had been overdue for lunch for a couple of hours.

As Dale had experienced before, long bouts of sensory deprivation sometimes resulted in hallucinatory perceptions and a disassociation with the passage of time.

Wait a second.

Quarter past three?

He was supposed to have heard about his promotion by now. By showing up this late at work, there was no chance of this promotion now. His boss had probably been frantically searching for him all afternoon. His hour-long excursion away from the office had lasted half of the day.

Oh boy.

Dale thumbed open his cell phone to check his voice mail.

☠   ☠   ☠

The air suddenly took on a sweet aftertaste.

"It's happening again," Robert Jacks muttered, feeling the orgasm-like sensations begin to flood through his body in tiny waves. "Another one joins."

Every newcomer always brought such sweet pleasure.

He moaned, trying to find the chair as his knees weakened.

Then came the distinct charbroiled taste of a hamburger covered in mozzarella cheese, with pickles and onions and a dab of honey mustard.

He moaned again, running his hands along his stomach and chest.

The acidy sweetness of an orange rang through his tongue.

"Oh . . ."

☠ ☠ ☠

"I guess I am starting to catch a cold," Dale said, putting down his champagne glass. "I can't even taste this at all."

"Oh, trust me, Dad," Linda said. "It's excellent."

He smiled at his only daughter, who, with a gentle face framed in small black curls, was becoming almost the mirror image of her mother. "I'm glad you approve."

"Well, thanks for bringing me here with you and Mom. I really needed this break from studying for my finals."

His face flushed as he was reminded about how dedicated Linda was to her education. "Any time, Pumpkin."

Linda blushed. "I wished you wouldn't call me that. I'm a grown woman, Dad."

"Aw, you've been my Pumpkin for twenty-five years now. You'll always be my little Pumpkin."

"Yeah, I guess I am." Linda looked at the people at the adjacent table. "Just not so loud, okay? When I'm a doctor, I don't want people to be calling me Doctor Pumpkin."

Pam returned to the table from the washroom, a playful glimmer in her eyes. "Is he calling you Pumpkin again?"

Linda nodded sheepishly.

"Guilty as charged," Dale said.

"Well, now that your father has had his turn embarrassing you, maybe this would be a good time to talk to him about . . . you know."

Dale looked at his daughter, his eyebrows lifted high.

"I was hoping to get myself a car."

"A car?"

"Yeah, well, I've been looking at this Impala for the past couple of weeks."

"And how are you going to pay for it?"

"With money, Dad."

"With what money?"

"With borrowed money."

Dale turned to Pam and winked so that his daughter couldn't see. "Honey, you're in Med school. I don't think the bank will lend a student the kind of money you need to buy a car."

"Daaad . . ." Linda rolled her eyes.

"Oh, sweetheart," Pam said. "Your father is just teasing you."

Moving his hand over his daughter's hair, Dale said. "We'll see what we can do, okay, Pumpkin? I'm not sure how much of a raise it is that I'm getting, but I'm sure that your mother and I will be able to manage something."

☠   ☠   ☠

Robert Jacks rolled his tongue across his lips.

Fine champagne. The finest he'd ever tasted. Then steak, cooked medium rare and smothered with onions and mushrooms. Baked potato covered in sour cream and bits of bacon – real bacon, not chips of simulated bacon flavor. Steamed clams. Orange crush. Hamburger. Cheese and macaroni. Peanut butter and strawberry jam on whole wheat bread. The hot bite of cheap whiskey.

Supper time was always the most difficult and the most satisfying. There was no accounting for some tastes. But, with a little effort, he could focus in on the right ones, the good ones.

He concentrated.

Had to block out the countless other sensations, focus on the good ones, the rich ones, the satisfying ones.

Ah, there it was. Champagne.

And another. "Mmm," Chocolate mousse.

☠   ☠   ☠

Getting out of the office early on Friday wasn't a problem, especially now that Dale was the one in charge of letting everyone go. There was a junior division baseball game that evening, and quite a few of the office staff had tickets for it. Being in a good mood because of his promotion and wanting to leave early himself, Dale gladly dismissed everyone two hours before their shifts ended.

But the worry that the added responsibility brought him had still been enough to tie his shoulder muscles into tense knots. And then there was the fact that, despite his promise to Linda, buying the car just wasn't possible. No matter how he and Pam had crunched the numbers, the money needed was simply not there, at least not for the next six months until they got on top of their bill payments.

By the time Dale was sinking into the sensory deprivation room at Jacks Health Club, he felt he needed it twice as badly as the last time he'd used it.

Like before, the darkness enveloped his sight immediately, the Muzak faded to silence and he was barely aware of the floor beneath his feet when he realized his sense of smell was already gone.

As before, he was left with the taste of darkness.

He rolled the pleasure of its light bitter-sweetness around on his tongue like some forbidden fruit. The taste was fleeting yet powerful. Like a shadow visible only in peripheral vision, one moment it was there, and the next it was gone. He relished in the sheer primordial experience of it.

Linda's car, he thought as the taste of the dark played over his taste buds. How can we get Linda's car for her? His mind carefully considered all the steps that he and Pam had taken to work out a car payment funding.

Slowly, his mind reeled over the dilemma, until finally it became nothing more than another thought, stirring no emotion, no worry, no fear, no tension.

It was simply a fact.

And facts could be dealt with.

Things would work out.

The bitter-sweet taste of the dark ensured that it would.

"I'm whipping up some bacon and eggs for Linda." Pam said as Dale entered the kitchen. "Would you like me to make some extra for you?"

"No thanks. Linda's here?"

"Yeah. She was in the neighborhood after the buses stopped running last night, so she crashed here instead of walking back to the dorm."

Dale pictured his daughter walking across the city in the middle of the night, alone and vulnerable. Within his imagination, at every corner, within every shadow, lurked some perverted maniac with a knife and a repressed hatred for young beautiful women.

"Everywhere I look, I'm reminded about how much more sense it makes that she should have a car. Anything could happen to her while walking home from the bus stop at night."

"I know, but we already tried to work something out."

"That doesn't make it any easier. Have you told her yet?"

"No. I thought we'd do it together."

Dale kissed the back of Pam's neck while reaching over her shoulder to grasp a strip of bacon from a plate between the elements of the stovetop.

She turned to kiss his cheek while he devoured the crispy strip. "I thought the smell of bacon frying would have you stampeding down here like wildfire. Are you sure you don't want some?"

Dale frowned. He hadn't actually smelled the bacon frying. And it tasted bland.

"No thanks. I'm not that hungry." He poured himself a cup of coffee and sat down at the kitchen table.

Pam walked over to feel his forehead. "You feeling okay?"

"I think the bug that I picked up is getting worse," he said, sipping the coffee without really being able to taste it. "Not only does everything taste funny, but I can't seem to smell anything either."

"You don't sound stuffed up."

"No, I'm not. It's strange. Last week my sense of taste seemed dulled but I could at least smell the things I was eating. But now I can't smell anything. I never realized how much of what we taste actually comes from smelling the food." He put the coffee down. "I've never had such a lifeless cup of coffee in my whole life."

"Well, thanks very much, Dad," Linda said, walking into the kitchen. "You used to like the way I made coffee."

"Pumpkin!" Dale's frown dissolved into a grin.

Linda kissed her father on the forehead as she dropped into the chair beside him. She threw a small stack of envelopes and flyers onto the table. "By the way, the mail's here."

Dale smiled at Linda. "Thanks. And by the way, I'm sure the coffee is just fine."

"Dad has a pretty nasty cold. Or flu. We're not sure."

"I can't taste or smell anything. But otherwise I feel fine." He fumbled through the envelopes, but one stuck out. Something official looking from VISA.

"Pam, didn't we pay our VISA bill last week?"

"Of course," Pam wiped her hands on the dish rag and reached for the envelope. "Why? Did they send us something?"

"Yup,"

She tore the envelope open with her thumb, pulled out the letter and started to read it aloud. "Dear Mr. Johnson. We are delighted to inform you that you are one of twelve winners selected in our "Buy and Win" promotion . . ." She paused, reading the rest in silence. "I don't believe it!" She brought the letter up to her nose and read the rest of the letter in silence. Her eyes shifted back and forth at a rate that was almost humorous.

"What?" Dale asked, beginning to get up.

"What is it, Mom?"

Pam dropped the letter on the table. "Congratulations, Linda. You're the proud owner of a brand-new Chevrolet Impala."

☠   ☠   ☠

Robert Jacks woke to the unmistakable smell of frying bacon and freshly brewed coffee.

The sensation hit him with an alarmingly refreshing jolt of pure pleasure.

He rolled across the bed and moaned in pleasure.

With every newcomer, with every sensation, the effect it had was not only increasingly additive, it was logarithmic in intensity.

He orgasmed as the rush of sensations flooded in.

☠   ☠   ☠

"Welcome back to Earth," Gail said.

Dale looked up at her and realized for the first time, that she must have been standing beside his desk for a few minutes already. "Oh. Hi, Gail."

"Is anything wrong? You've seemed distracted all week. We're kind of worried about you."

Dale fidgeted with his pen, considering revealing to her the strange things he had been mulling over, then gingerly placed the pen down on his desk and forced a smile.

"Honest, Gail, it's nothing. Just this cold that I can't seem to shake. It has me a little on edge, is all. I haven't been grumpy all week, have I?"

"No. Just distracted. You sure you're okay?"

Dale nodded. "Besides this cold, I've never been better. And that's the truth." He surveyed the office and noticed that everyone else was gone. He glanced at his watch. It was a few minutes shy of 6 PM. "It looks like the weekend has already started. Why don't you start enjoying it?"

"Sure," Gail began to make her way to the door.

"And, Gail?"

She paused, turning.

"Thanks for the concern."

She smiled and nodded, then walked out the door.

Leaving Dale to speculate about the events of the past couple of weeks.

He couldn't help but wonder about the sensory deprivation room. He'd joined the new health club because he needed a place to unwind after a hard day at work. The sensory deprivation room had been an added bonus, providing him with a place to meditate about his worries and problems. And, so far, every problem that he'd brought into the room had been solved in some way.

The promotion he could see as a coincidence, because it was something he'd been working at all along, something he had earned.

But the Impala.

He couldn't ignore that.

It was difficult to believe that he and Pam had inadvertently won a brand-new car through the credit card company simply by charging more than five hundred dollars on it and being automatically entered in a contest. Not only was it a new car, but it was the exact model that Linda had been hoping for.

The coincidence was too convenient to ignore.

Something had to be going on.

But what?

Slowly, Dale got up from the desk, deciding it was time to pay Mr. Jacks another visit, and perhaps get some answers.

        ☠   ☠   ☠

"Twelve more clients signed on today," Robert Jacks whispered, pacing across the office of his health club. "Making it . . . fifty this week. Fifty!"

A grin shot up his face, and he struggled with the incoming scents and tastes. Fixing his jaw tight, he pushed them out. He had to keep them out for at least a few minutes. He had to be allowed a few moments to think, instead of just feel, just sense.

If the sensation with just three clients was great before, he was about to reach an ecstasy like one he'd never felt before.

And that was merely the beginning.

Because, once they discovered the power of the room, they got greedy. They wanted more. They would trade anything for what they desired.

And the deeper they traded, the more heightened each acquired sense became.

Just before the sensations overpowered his concentration, Robert Jacks thought about what it would be like to feel, taste, smell, hear, and see through every single client.

It was just a matter of time.

Just a matter of recurring visits.

☠   ☠   ☠

Dale's cell phone rang just as he reached the office door.

"Hello?"

"Dale?" Even though it was strained and weak, he recognized his wife's voice.

"Pam. What's wrong? What happened?"

"I'm so scared, Dale."

"What happened, hon? Just tell me what happened."

"There was . . . an accident."

☠   ☠   ☠

Turning away from the bed, Dale buried his face between Pam's neck and shoulder. He could no longer stand to look at the twisted body of his daughter, at the tubes and needles that ran amok about her, at the deep dark circles around eyes that stared back at him, empty.

"Pumpkin . . ." Dale could barely choke out the word.

"She'll be okay," Pam said. "The doctor says that there's still a chance she could come out of it."

That's not enough, Dale thought. That's just not enough. Linda was trapped in a hell worse than death. Even though he no longer looked at her, he could still see her lying as if prisoner to the bed and the machines that kept her alive, still hear the machine that forced air in and out of her lungs in asthmatic sounding breaths, and the digital beep of her heartbeat, keeping the beat to the horrific tune of life support.

"This can't be happening," Dale said, his words hitching as he cried.

Pam's arms came around him as he wept. He was barely aware of the soothing pattern his wife's hands made as they rubbed along his back.

For an obscure second, the distant feel of Pam's hands reminded him of another place, another time.

Another possibility.

The feeling of what it was like to lose the very sense of touch.

And suddenly it became clear. The whole twisted notion made sense. He sacrificed his sense of taste and received a promotion. He gave up his sense of smell and in return was awarded a new car.

It wasn't crazy. It wasn't stupid. It was the most logical thing that could happen. Perhaps that was what Mr. Jacks meant when he said his visit to the room had already been paid for. He was paying for each visit and resolution with the loss of a sense.

"You scratch my back, and I'll scratch yours," Dale whispered. The ultimate deal.

"What's that?" Pam asked.

Dale didn't answer. Teary eyed, he looked up at his wife and smiled. There was hope after all. Mr. Jacks was about to have his back scratched, in spades.

☠ ☠ ☠

This time it felt like the flood would never stop. Robert Jacks could do nothing but roll about on the floor and let the sensations consume him.

They had to work their way through his mind, through his very soul, and then, maybe then, he would attempt to control them again.

But in the meantime, he was too busy enjoying the ecstasy.

He'd never experienced multiple orgasms before.

☠ ☠ ☠

Dale stepped into the room, and, like the times before, welcomed the darkness as it enveloped his senses, one by one.

But, unlike the times before, as his five senses were enveloped in darkness he was aware of the power that flowed through that darkness. The power that was the unknown sense. That other sense the room allowed him to tap into. The sense of the foundation of the universe. The sense that could manipulate the fabric of reality. And this time, he was prepared to give anything, prepared to make any sacrifice, for the life of his daughter.

Dale's first visit to the room had taken a few hours, the second visit twice as long.

This time, Dale was prepared to stay forever, trade his entire being, if that was what was required.

He thought about his daughter, body twisted and pinned to the bed like some insect that was under study. Her every vital sign was displayed for the entire room to see. Her body was vulnerable to the whim of anyone who came along.

And her eyes. They stared out into nothing.

No, not nothing. The darkness. They stared into the very realm of darkness that enveloped Dale.

He concentrated on Linda. Searched through the darkness until he found where she was looking. Her eyes, void of the very life, the utter sunshine that used to radiate from them, were empty, staring into the darkness and seeking death. Dale was able to grab her focus, manipulate it.

Linda had to live, she had to survive. She was better than this even that had occurred, stronger that this damage that had been done to her body. She would endure, and emerge victorious.

As his mind whirled, orbited around his daughter's consciousness and the intense power of the dark, the feeling that there was a floor beneath him began to dissolve completely.

Something pulled at him, at his very soul, and his body went with it. He spun through the darkness, somehow aware that he was moving at a breakneck speed. Something else pulled at him, snapped him back the way he had come. Then again.

It was like a fishing line, pulling at him, but not wanting the entire weight of him, only wanting to select a piece of him. He wouldn't have any of it, forcing himself, giving himself entirely to the darkness. He was pulled forward and snapped back more again and again.

The repeated back and forth struggle took everything in him to stay focused on his single pursuit and desire.

An eternity seemed to pass as his will battled with the powers of the dark.

In time, the sense of time actually passing was gone. There was only his spirit and the darkness, engaged in an endless see-saw struggle.

He floated on, aware only that his senses had been snatched from his body.

And then there was nothing.

Nothing but Linda.

Nothing but a glimmer of life in her eyes, a twitch of her lips as she croaked out a desire for water.

Dale felt himself finally dissipate into the darkness, become one with it, secure in the knowledge that his daughter would be all right. The power needed to see his goal completed seemed to have taken more than his senses – it required the absorption of his entire being. He let it happen, molecule by molecule he allowed himself to be given up to the darkness.

Then, a great sensation of brightness struck.

He was blinded by it, but somehow also deafened and burnt. In an obscure way, he could smell and taste the intensity of the brightness.

And then there was nothing again.

His mind reeled, and he was aware of the floor again, aware that he was falling over. The floor rushed up and struck the side of his head.

He let out a moan that was consumed by the darkness around him.

Stumbling to his feet, he began to run, unsure of why he was running, of where he was running to.

Then he ran into something solid.

And lost consciousness.

A strange moaning sound invaded Dale's ears. He rolled over, feeling as if his body were one giant bruise. There was a faint smell of fresh paint and the stale air had never tasted so joyous.

Slowly, Dale cracked opened his eyes to find himself in the unlit, darkened hallway of Jacks Health Club. He turned to see that the sensory deprivation room no longer existed. There was a plain solid wall there. No darkened entrance.

He got to his feet and listened. The moaning came from the other side of Mr. Jacks' closed office door. The moaning was muffled, but it wasn't just because it came from the other side of a door. It was as if a wad of cotton were stuffed in Dales' ears.

As he looked up he realized that the lights in the hallway were on. It just seemed like all the sixty watt bulbs had been replaced by ten watt bulbs.

He had all his senses back, but they seemed to be muted. Damaged.

But along with that loss came the experience of another sense. The one he'd experienced in the darkness. The one that had allowed him to sense the fabric of reality, and to manipulate it. With that sense, he was able to determine that Jacks had tapped into the power of the darkness and been using it, and the average person's selfish desires to negotiate a metaphysical trade and ultimately covet senses from his clients.

The moaning from the office became static and turned into a high-pitched wail.

Dale opened the door to see Mr. Jacks lying on the floor, his entire body quivering as if he were trapped in an eternal epileptic seizure. The wail changed back into a moan, then converted into a repeated babble, from which Dale could make out only two words.

Too much.

Somewhere, some place in the back of his mind, the dark sense allowed Dale to understand what had happened. When Dale had forced the trade of all the rest of his senses too quickly, Jacks was forced to deal with more powerful sensations at once than his mind could handle.

Jacks' ultimate voyeuristic vicarious experiences were finally over.

Like a computer that ran out of system resources, Jacks had been unable to handle any more input, overloaded and crashed.

Leaving the man to his over-sensed hell, Dale left the office. He would deal with his newly acquired sense later. His only concern for the moment was to get back to the hospital and welcome his Pumpkin back to the world of the living.

Little Things

ONE NIGHT DANIEL Jackson woke to the sound of a quiet tapping noise coming from the ceiling above his bed.

"Joy, do you hear that?" he whispered to his wife.

"Hear what?" she mumbled, half-asleep.

"That tapping."

"You're dreaming. Go back to sleep."

He let it pass without mention when the tapping continued the next evening.

After several nights of the persistent little tapping noise he started getting used to it. He'd lie in bed and listen to it, the tapping becoming a soothing sound which relaxed him to sleep in a manner that no relaxation CD ever could.

One night, though, he awoke with an odd sense that something was wrong.

He looked at his clock radio. It was just after two in the morning. His wife was breathing softly beside him; he could hear the furnace gentling humming through the air ducts. Things seemed to be normal. He was about to drift off again when he realized what it was that was different.

The tapping had stopped.

A fine layer of dust particles settled on his face and he wiped it away and peered up at the ceiling. The ensuite bathroom light which they always left on during the night lent him a generous portion of light –- enough that he could make out a small hole, about the size of a dime, in the ceiling just above his head.

He sat up and peered more closely.

A tiny face peered at him through the hole.

Then something small fell from the hole, bounced lightly off of his shoulder and landed on his lap.

Daniel looked at it, his mouth dry and hanging open.

A tiny naked man, hairless except for a long flowing white beard and no more than an inch high, stood on Daniel's thigh and looked at him. He was holding what looked like a miniature pick axe. Had the tapping sound he'd heard been made by the little man's axe tunneling through the ceiling?

Daniel smiled as he looked down at the man. It was as if he were gazing at a small kitten instead of an impossibly shrunken little naked man who had fallen through his ceiling in the middle of the night.

The little man smiled back at him, his eyes shiny little pin points of light set in his face.

His wife, Joy, rolled over.

"Honey, you okay?" she asked sleepily.

"Uh, yes dear," Still stunned, he didn't know what to say to her. Would she be unable to perceive the little man, just like she'd been unable to hear the tapping? "I just got up to go to the bathroom."

"Mmm. G'night." She rolled back over.

Daniel stared down at the little man who had started when he'd heard Joy's voice. Now he held the tiny axe high over his head and jumped off Daniel's thigh onto the bed.

The little figure stumbled over the rippled sheets, made his way over to Joy and swung the tiny axe into the flesh at the back of her neck.

Joy didn't react to the blow even though it made a small pin prick in her skin. The little man pulled the axe out and a tiny bead of blood appeared. The tiny man looked back over his shoulder at Daniel and smiled. Then he leaned forward and put his face up close to the bead of blood. After a moment, he turned back around and smiled at Daniel, his teeth offering a white contrast as he grinned a broad, blood caked smile.

Then, the little man took a running leap, grabbed onto Joy's hair, and pulled himself into the depths of her curly locks.

Daniel sat there for an indeterminable amount of time, looking at the point where the little man had disappeared, waiting for him to appear again. But he didn't. Eventually, Daniel fell asleep, lying on his side and staring at the back of Joy's head.

☠   ☠   ☠

"You didn't sleep well last night, did you?" Joy asked, looking up from her morning newspaper at the breakfast table.

Daniel finished his coffee and stared back at her, saying nothing.

"Are you okay, hon'?"

He got up, poured himself another cup of coffee, then sat back down at the table.

"Hon'?"

"Yeah, I'm Okay, Joy. I guess I didn't sleep very well at all." He didn't know what to say to her about what he'd seen last night. *Joy, last night I found out what had been making that little tapping noise. It was a tiny little man with a pick axe. He popped out of the ceiling, stabbed you in the back of the neck and drank your blood.* If he told her that not only would she not believe him, but she'd have him committed. It was such a zany memory that he knew it had to have been a dream. But he just couldn't bring himself to tell her about it. He nervously chuckled.

"Dan? What's so funny?"

He didn't respond. Instead, he thought back to how he'd laid awake staring at Joy's head, and knew it couldn't have been a dream. That was why he'd been so afraid to tell Joy about it. Because it really had happened.

Joy looked down into his coffee cup. "I've never seen you take your coffee black before. You're acting really strange. Are you sure you're not feeling sick?"

"No. No, I'm fine. I . . ."

The little man emerged from Joy's hair, scaled down the side of her head, leapt to her shoulder and waved at Daniel.

Daniel stared at him.

"Dan! Something's wrong with you. You look pale all of a sudden." Joy said, getting up. Her movement sent the little man completely off balance and he tottered off the back of her shoulder, out of sight again.

Joy walked around the table to feel her husband's forehead.

Daniel scanned the floor, looking for where the little man had fallen.

"You don't feel feverish, but we shouldn't take any chances. I'll tell you what. We both take the day off work and I'll drive you up to see the doctor."

There was no sign of the little man on the floor. He looked back up at his wife. "No, Joy. Look, I'm fine. Okay?" He got up from the table and went to the washroom, slamming the door behind him.

Splashing cold water on his face he could hear her on the other side of the door expressing her concern and complaining about the way he was acting. He stood there, the bathroom door locked, listening to the sound of her voice, bothered by the high-pitched sound of it.

He waited, saying nothing back to her until she finally gave up and left for work.

☠   ☠   ☠

That evening as Daniel read in bed, he listened to the sounds of his wife showering, deciding he would try to make it up to her.

The shower stopped. Joy walked out of the bathroom, her naked skin glistening, her eyes playful.

"How do you feel right now?" she asked.

He put down the book and admired her. For a woman approaching her mid-forties, Joy was still in excellent shape. Her breasts had retained all the shape and perkiness they had had eighteen years ago when he'd first seen her naked. His eyes wandered down her taunt stomach, past her dark patch of pubic hair and along her long, luscious legs. He admired the tanned, well-toned legs, remembering her high school nickname: *Gams*. She'd been a sprinter for the high school track and field team and had continued running all these years; likely one of the reasons her body still looked so trim, so toned.

"I feel great, now," he said. Pulling his covers aside he revealed the extent of his excitement to her.

Joy's smile intensified as she slid over to the bed and mounted him.

Their eyes fixed on each other lovingly as she slowly moved herself up and down.

No more words were spoken. They continued to gaze at each other, never breaking eye contact. He lifted a hand up to softly caress a breast.

As his hand slid around the side of her left breast, Daniel felt a sudden pin prick on his pinky. He withdrew it suddenly.

"Ouch!"

She stopped her rhythmic movement and leaned forward. "What's wrong, hon?"

As she leaned forward, Daniel could see the little tiny man clinging to the side of her breast where he had felt the stab of pain. It was the same one he'd seen the night before. The little man had gouged out a section of flesh on her side behind her breast about the size of a penny.

Daniel looked up into Joy's eyes. She obviously could not feel it. Then, beyond her, the movement of a shadow brought his eyes to the hole in the ceiling again. Something else was crawling out of it. It fell out, the same way the little man had the night before, and landed on Joy's head. It was another tiny man. Naked, white flowing beard, a pick axe in its hand.

"Dan? Answer me!"

"Jesus Christ!" he yelled, scrambling out from under her. "Why can't you feel it?" He fled from the bedroom.

"Dan? What the hell is wrong?" She got up and went after him, meeting him in the hall. He was standing in the hall looking confused and rather silly as he paced back and forth, his slowly subsiding erection bobbing as he walked.

"Dan. What is it? Why can't I feel *what*? Why won't you make love to me?"

"What?" He looked at her, hearing her words and seeing the two identical figures on her body. The first one still on the side of her breast, the second one swinging his axe down into the top of her head.

"Why did you stop? Did I do something wrong?"

"No, Joy, it isn't you." He had trouble forming the words while watching the little creatures. "There's this . . . there are these . . . things. Shit, Joy, I don't know how to tell you, how to explain."

"Then what is it?" She looked at him in silence and then her eyes widened in horror. For a moment, he thought she could finally detect what was happening to her – finally perceive the little men. Then she spoke. "You're having an affair! You're cheating on me! Is that it?"

"No! Dammit, Joy! No!" The little man on her breast was clawing his way across the front of her breast and started biting her nipple.

"It's true, isn't it? You *are* having an affair."

Daniel watched, dumbfounded, as the little man chewed the tip of her nipple off. "No!" He lunged forward and swatted her left breast, sending the little man hurling through the air across the hallway.

"You bastard!" Joy punched Daniel in the mouth, smashing his lip against his teeth, then kicked him in the shin and he dropped to his knees, hands held to his bleeding lip. "You've got a lot of nerve." She opened her mouth to say more but then turned, went back into the bedroom and slammed the door.

Daniel looked for the little man and saw him sitting, stunned, up against the opposite wall. He shook his little head and then quickly got to his feet, dashed across the rug and scrambled under the door into the bedroom.

"Joy!" Daniel screamed, helplessly. "Joy!"

He heard the bedroom door locking.

"Joy. Please. I don't know how to explain. I don't know how to tell you . . ."

"You've told me enough already for one night. Leave me alone, Dan. Just leave me the fuck alone."

☠   ☠   ☠

The next morning, Daniel woke in the bed in the guest room, the room they'd originally slated to be the baby's room when they first bought the house – the room that, despite years of trying to conceive, was still a guest room. Spending the night there had been a double slap in the face. He didn't get out of bed until he heard Joy leaving for work. This would be the second day in a row that he would be late for his own job, a fact which his boss didn't let go unnoticed.

Daniel reached for the phone and considered calling in sick, but decided he needed to get to work just to take his mind off these new developments. If he let it really sink in, he simply wouldn't be able to deal with it.

He got up and went to the master bedroom. He made it as far as the doorway and stood there, stunned.

Little bits of flesh and droplets of blood were scattered all over the bedroom floor. The unmade bed was covered in blood and more tiny chunks of flesh.

What the hell had they done to her?

Daniel got dressed without having a shower and left the house without eating. He drove straight to Joy's place of work, double parked in front of the office building and hurried inside.

The elevator opened at the floor where Joy's office was, and he stepped out and scanned the room. Things seemed their normal bustle of activity for a daily metropolitan paper. It was sectioned off into little cubicles where reporters worked diligently at their various stories and assignments. Little did they know they had one hell of a story right under their noses.

Daniel walked past the cubicled area to the glass encased office of the assistant managing sports editor, Joy Mavitz. He approached the glass slowly and peeked in.

Joy's back was turned to him. She was speaking to someone on the phone. Like the reporters, she seemed to be having a typical day. Then she turned to pick up a file on her desk, and Daniel let out a gasp.

The left side of her face was missing huge sections of flesh. He could see clean through to her skull in several areas.

Hanging from a string of her hair, a little man was digging into her forehead with a pick axe. Another one, this one tubby and with a much longer beard was sitting in a gouge in her cheek, scratching out the flesh above him in a lackadaisical fashion like a bored worker casually scratching his ass during an extra long coffee break. A third one appeared from the sleeve of her blouse, carrying a huge hunk of flesh twice his size. He chewed part of it, then threw it onto the desk. It landed on the file Joy was reading, but she didn't seem to notice.

Another one poked out from under the neckline of her blouse on the opposite side, and was joined by a second little man. They began working together at a flap of skin that hung down from her jaw. Yet another one climbed out of a tangle of her hair and joined them.

Daniel stood there with his mouth hanging open. They had multiplied.

And they were stripping her of her skin. They were excavating her flesh; mining her body.

☠   ☠   ☠

"Another beer?"

Daniel looked up at Jake, the owner and bartender of *Jake's Place*, a small tavern at the west end of the city. Across the street from Daniel's place of work, he had frequented the bar for close to fifteen years.

Daniel regarded Jake as the closest friend he had even though this bar was the only place they ever saw each other.

"Yeah, Jake. And a shot of rye, too."

Jake took the empty beer mug with one hand and filled it under the tap, letting the foam drip over the top, then reached behind him and topped up a shot glass with whiskey.

"You really gonna divorce her?" Jake asked as he slid the two filled glasses toward Daniel.

"Yeah. Yeah, I think so." Daniel downed the shot and chased it with half of his beer. "I think that would be best."

"You mind if I ask you something?" Jake took the shot glass and dropped it into the sudsy water of a little sink behind the bar.

"Sure,"

"Well, if I remember correctly, you and Joy have been married for a long time."

"Yeah, about twelve years."

"I remember the first time you brought her here, too. Two young lovebirds, couldn't take your eyes, or your hands off each other."

Daniel closed his eyes and smiled at the memory.

"A few years later, you two got married. And, as expected, there were problems along the way. You had the typical things a couple argues about. Money, the bills, work getting in the way of your relationship. Even the struggle of trying so desperately to have kids but not being able to, despite all the tests from the doctors showing there wasn't a reason for it."

At that memory, Daniel brought the beer mug to his lips and took a long draw from it.

Jake scooped up the shot glass from the soapy sink water and absently dried it while he continued. "Oh sure, you came in here from time to time just to get away and talk whenever you had a major fight.

"But never once did you consider leaving her. Never once did that become an option. Never once did you fail to inform me of the fact that you and Joy loved each other and *that* was what made all the difference. That's what you always said to me.

"So what happened? What changed?"

Daniel regarded Jake with the compassion of a patient looking at the surgeon who had saved his life. In many ways, over the years, Jake had been a life saver. Just having him to bounce his troubles off of, to hear him out had always helped Jake through the most troubling of times.

He felt he owed Jake something.

Over the years Jake had been a supportive figure in Daniel's life. Jake had been witness to the many ups and downs of Daniel's marriage. And he was right. Daniel and Joy *had* gone through a lot together and always came out stronger.

But this time, it was different. *Really* different. And Jake, a man who had been long devoted to listening to Daniel's stories, deserved some sort of explanation.

Daniel took another sip of his beer and set it down again in the exact same ring mark on the coaster.

"I love her, Jake. I always have. I still do. I knew she wasn't perfect, just as she knew the same about me. And I loved her, knowing that. Our marriage has crumbled rather quickly in just a couple of days; the relationship has ceased to work, but I know a part of me will always love Joy.

"If I tried to explain to you exactly why I had to leave her, you wouldn't listen. As good a friend as you've been to me, I know for sure that if I told you the details, I'd lose your sympathetic ear – that you simply wouldn't listen. And I wouldn't blame you because I'm still having trouble sorting those details in my own mind."

The image of Joy as he last saw her struck him. He saw her quite clearly, sitting at her desk, unaware of the handful of tiny creatures as they mined the flesh from her body.

Daniel looked down into his beer and smiled a bitter smile. "Let's just suffice it to say that after all these years, after all we've been through, it was the Little Things that changed it all.

"No matter how much I still love my wife, I just couldn't live with the Little Things."

The Pizza Man

CARL WAS HOVERING on the edge of consciousness when he became aware of the faint smell of pepperoni, tomato sauce and cheese. It was just strong enough to make him realize how long it had been since he'd had a filling meal.

And though physically exhausted – having spent the day moving into the old two story brownstone just a few blocks away from the university – the scent of the pizza kept luring him by the stomach and slowly pulling him out of his sleep.

Carl's first conscious thought was of a jealous annoying nature. Sure, he was grateful that his cousin Rick, now in his second year of university, had allowed him to move into the newly rented four-bedroom home with two of his classmates, the very lovely Nancy and Marty. But Carl was a freshman, completely new to town and living "on his own" and still felt a bit like an outsider among the small group of four.

The thought that Rick and the girls had ordered a late-night pizza without waking and inviting him to join them just added to that sense of being an outsider.

There was a rustling outside his bedroom door and he sat up in the bed, now fully awake. The smell of pizza seemed stronger and although he couldn't see the door of his room as it opened he could hear the slight whispered sigh as it moved.

Because there didn't seem to be any lights on in the rest of the house – not even a sliver of light coming from down the stairs – a shiver spread through Carl and he felt an immediate surge of goose bumps swelling on his arms.

He instinctively reached for where the bed lamp had been back in his bedroom in his parents' home; but finding no light to turn on, no sense of familiar security to grasp, released a quiet whimper.

Through the darkness he heard a muted whispering from just inside his doorway and he gripped the sheets in fear. His eyes had become more accustomed to the dimly lit room and he could start to make out a figure standing in the doorway. A short figure.

"Carl?" It was a female voice. His panic quickly subsided as he recognized the voice and stature. It was Marty, the tiny girl with the long dark curly hair and big green eyes. Though he couldn't see her in the dark, his mind harkened back to how he'd spent much of that day when they were all moving furniture into the house gazing longingly at Marty's smooth, sun-browned legs and how her breasts strained against the confines of her t-shirt with the efforts of lifting and unpacking boxes.

And now here she was in his room. More goose bumps filled his arms, but for a different reason. Here was this beautiful, sexy girl, now in his bedroom in the middle of the night.

"Yeah?"

"Do you smell that pizza?" She found the light switch and turned it on.

Carl covered his eyes, squinting at her through his hands. "Uh-huh. Are Rick and Nancy cooking downstairs?"

"No," she said. "There's no light coming from down there. And besides, we don't have the ingredients to make a pizza."

There was a soft knock at the front door which carried clearly up the stairs and into Carl's room.

"What time is it?" Carl asked.

"Quarter to one,"

They waited in silence, staring at each other. There was another soft knock.

"Is someone gonna get that?" Rick yelled sleepily from his bedroom. "And while you're at it, keep it down, you two."

Carl hopped out of bed and his face flushed – he'd momentarily forgotten he was wearing only his underwear. He quickly grabbed his house coat from where it sat piled at the foot of his bed.

He headed down the stairs with Marty close behind him. They crept down in the dark and when they reached the bottom, headed down the hall toward the front door. As they got closer, Carl felt along the wall for the switch to the outside light and flicked it on.

The front porch light came on to reveal a dark figure backlit in the door window, a pizza box held high in his left hand.

The knock sounded once more, this time urgently.

The smell of tomato sauce and pepperoni was stronger than before as Carl stepped closer to the door. The figure was easier to make out now. Carl could see it was a male; a blond teenager with a few thick red pimples and a striking solid cleft chin. And even though he shouldn't have been able to see through the glass and into the darkened hall, his blue eyes seemed to follow Carl and Marty as they moved closer to the door.

"Pizza?" Carl asked through the closed door.

"Large pepperoni and mushroom,"

Carl opened the door. The smell of pizza was even stronger and more tantalizing. Carl heard his stomach rumble in response. He wanted this pizza, mistake or not.

"What's the damage?"

"Thirteen fifty," the blond teenager flashed a white toothy grin at Marty.

"I'll be right back," Carl said, turning to sprint up the stairs to get his wallet. When he got upstairs he found his wallet still in the back pocket of the jeans he'd thrown into the pile of clothes at the foot of his bed. He was just pulling the wallet out when he heard Marty scream.

      ☠   ☠   ☠

"Are you sure you weren't sleepwalking?" Rick asked, lying in his bed facing the wall. Carl, Marty and Nancy were all standing in his bedroom doorway.

"She couldn't have been," Carl said. "We told you: I was there too. I saw him. Besides, you heard the knock yourself."

"All right. All right." Rick rolled over to face them. "You go downstairs. There's a pizza guy at the door. No one ordered a pizza. So far, no big deal. Mistakes happen, right?

"So Carl goes to get some money. Marty feels a draft, so asks the pizza guy to step inside. She steps around to close the door and when she turns around she can't see him. He's not there."

Trembling, Marty looked at the floor. "He vanished. Just like that. Gone."

"Look," Rick said. "People can't just vanish into thin air. It's impossible."

"Then what happened, Rick?" Carl placed a reassuring hand on Marty's shoulder. "When I heard Marty's scream I ran back downstairs and found Marty passed out in the hallway. The door was open and the pizza guy was gone."

Nancy nodded vigorously. Upon hearing Marty's scream, she had bounded out of bed, followed Carl downstairs and helped him revive Marty.

"Listen to yourselves," Rick said. "All the evidence is there that he *didn't* vanish. Here's what probably happened, Marty. When you turned around and couldn't see him he was probably standing in your blind spot. And then you freaked out, screamed and fainted." He paused to smirk. "And you scared the hell out of him. What would you do in his situation if some stranger asked you to step into their house at one in the morning and then turned around and screamed at you? You'd get the hell out of there, wouldn't you?"

"That does make sense," Nancy said. "Because the door was open. He must have been scared and ran off after Marty fainted."

They stood in Rick's room for a few minutes, reassuring themselves that everything was okay until Rick said that enough was enough, get out of his room so he could get back to sleep.

☠   ☠   ☠

During the rest of the night Carl slept restlessly. He kept hearing a soft knocking at the door and was positive by the odor in the air that someone had brought a freshly cooked pizza into the house. A few times during the night, Marty called out from her room that she heard a noise downstairs. Just as many times Rick yelled out for her to shut up and get back to sleep.

☠   ☠   ☠

When Carl opened the fridge to get himself and his three housemates a fresh round of beer, a partially torn and half-faded sticker caught his eye. Sure, he'd seen it yesterday, but suddenly something about the red graphic on it – the chubby man with a beard holding a steaming pizza – had a new familiarity to it.

He'd seen that same graphic on the pizza box the blond teenager had brought to the door the night before. The faded letters *Jimbo's Pizza* were still readable on the sticker as was the phone number.

It wasn't difficult convincing the rest of the house mates that ordering a pizza was a good idea, particularly since it had been four hours since they'd had supper: Their fine gourmet meal of hot dog wieners with a side of macaroni and cheese.

Inspired by the disappearing pizza guy from the night before, Carl suggested they order a large pepperoni and mushroom.

"It'll be here in half an hour or it's free," Carl said as he stood in the entranceway to the living room. "And it comes to fourteen twenty-five. C'mon, pony up the dough."

They all flipped their beer caps at him in response.

Carl couldn't help smiling. This was exactly how he'd imagined moving away and going to university would be; fun, freedom, playful adventure and -- his eyes settled momentarily on Marty, on the cute wrinkle in the corner of her eyes as she flipped another beer cap at him -- hanging out with gorgeous women.

Once they ran out of beer caps they started figuring out how to divide the cost of the pizza. It was easiest to round up, with tip, to sixteen dollars so they could each contribute four.

Carl had settled back down on a milk crate propped up beside the armchair Marty was sitting in and was about to ask about her home town, try to determine if there was a boyfriend back there, when there was a soft knock at the door.

Holding the money he collected, Carl got up and rounded the corner to the front door. The blond-haired teen from the night before smiled uneasily at him as the door opened. His blue eyes seemed a little more sunken and his face was quite paler than the previous night.

The pizza guy smiled at him. "Large pepperoni and mushroom. Thirteen fifty."

Carl took the pizza box and, having been ready with the sixteen dollars, turned and took a half step back to shoot a confused look at his room-mates. "It comes to thirteen fifty?"

"I thought you said it was fourteen twenty-five?" Rick asked.

Carl shrugged and turned back to the door.

The young blond was no longer standing in the doorway.

He stepped forward, peered out the door and was greeted by a soft September wind. The dark street was empty of both cars and pedestrians. He closed the door and went back into the living room with the pizza.

"Looks like this one is free," he said.

Hungry and drawn to the scent oozing from the box, they gathered on the floor around the pizza box. Rick tore cheesy pieces off and handed them around, nibbling on the strings of cheese from each one.

Marty shifted her piece from hand to hand. "Oh! Hot!"

Nancy sank her teeth in, starting to make the low satisfied moan of enjoying the taste. The moan quickly changed in pitch to a startled yelp and she threw the pizza slice into the air.

It landed face up on the carpet and the layer of cheese seemed to slide about on its own. A large beetle peered out from under the cheese and then scurried quickly beneath the sofa.

Marty dropped her slice and screamed as a cockroach hopped off her slice and scuttled down her arm. Rick quickly swatted it off and it hurried to join the beetle under the sofa.

"What the hell?" Carl mumbled, throwing his piece against the wall. It landed crust-up and a pair of bugs quickly ran from beneath it to hide under the armchair.

Rick dropped his slice into the box as they all jumped to their feet. The pizza still left untouched seemed to be slithering around in the box. The cheese moved as if the surface were a liquid on a tilting, rotating surface.

"Geeziz," Rick said, spitting out the bits of cheese he'd been chewing, and threw up. He stayed bent over, not quite finished and barfed again. Nancy joined him for the second round.

Rick, still green in the face, wiped his mouth and looked up at Carl, who was about to contribute the contents of his own stomach to the mess on the floor.

There was a loud knock on the door.

"Oh my god!" Marty yelled and leaned forward, retching.

Rick went to the door and Carl followed, pausing to flip the top of the pizza box closed.

The door opened and a dark haired middle aged man with an unsightly amount of pock-marks on his face stood holding an insulated pizza bag at waist level.

"Jimbo's pizza," he mumbled. "Large pepperoni and mushroom. That'll be fourteen twenty-five."

☠   ☠   ☠

The second pizza sat on the kitchen table uneaten.

Rick had taken a knife through it and discovered no roaches or bugs of any kind, dead or alive. Nonetheless, not a single one of them had any appetite. They simply stared at each other across the table.

"I don't understand it," Marty said, the green in her face almost completely gone.

"What does it mean?" Rick asked.

Carl got up and went down the hall to the living room. He came back with the bill that had been stapled to the first pizza box.

"What's that for?" Nancy asked, laying her head on Rick's shoulder. Rick stroked her short blonde hair.

"Take a close look," Carl said, "at the date penciled in. It says the fourth of September. But today is the third. And look at the year. It's last year's date."

Rick grabbed the bill from him and studied it. Then he looked at the bill on the pizza box on the table. "Today's date. Proper day, proper year."

"So we have three conflicting bits of information. The price, the day and the year. I'll bet if we called *Jimbo's* we might learn something more."

"Like what?" Rick asked.

"I'm not sure, but there has to be some explanation. Rick, why don't you call Jimbo's?"

"Why?"

"Well, we did receive a *defective* pizza from them."

Rick's eyes lit up and he got up from the table and picked up the phone. "You're right! They owe us." He dialed the number, told the person what happened and then described the delivery person.

"No," he said into the phone. "This isn't a joke."

His face went white and his mouth opened silently as he listened. He paused and then hung up the phone without saying another word.

"What?"

"According to the guy on the phone, this blond-haired kid disappeared in our neighborhood one year ago tomorrow. He's presumed dead, but his body has never been found."

☠   ☠   ☠

Carl sat up in his bed, startled awake.

Was that a noise downstairs?

He carefully flipped away the covers and went to the door, flicking on his bedroom light.

A sudden blue flash lit the room as the switch clicked on, and then the room quickly receded back into darkness. He stood there, blinded and momentarily confused.

Of all the times for the bulb to die.

Grumbling, he stumbled in the dark over to his desk and lit the room with his small desk lamp, creating an eerie shadowy landscape of his bedroom.

Looking over at his digital clock, he saw it was 1:30 AM. He stuck his head out the bedroom door and confirmed that everyone else was sleeping by the fact that there was no light appearing at the cracks on the bottom of their doors.

He went back into his room, slipped back under the sheets and began reading the paperback sitting on his night stand.

Though his eyes passed over the words he wasn't actually reading them. Instead, his mind was going over the details he'd found when researching online about the teenage pizza boy's disappearance the previous year.

His name was Steve Buick. He was eighteen and had been working at Jimbo's Pizza for only 6 months when a call into this same neighborhood had been the last time he'd ever been seen. He simply disappeared, and his abandoned car was found in a nearby parking lot.

Carl had found four or five archived articles online from two of the local newspapers, but nothing after that. No indication of the teenager being found, either dead or alive.

He must have fallen asleep because the next thing he knew was being startled awake some time later upon hearing a noise – one he could only imagine as a bony elbow bumping against wooden paneling.

This time he left the bedroom and decided to head down the stairs, deciding not to wake anyone else up. He noticed a sliver of light appear under Marty's door as soon as he stepped on the stair second from the top and making a gritting moan of shifting wood.

So he wasn't the only one who had awakened.

He waited for her door to open and her head to appear and looked at her from the stairs with an *it's only me* smile. She smiled back sleepily.

"Did you hear that noise?" she asked.

He nodded. "I'm going to check it out."

"Why don't you wake up Rick?"

"No," he smiled. "Not after last night. He'll probably clobber me if I disturb his beauty rest. Tell you what; if I don't come back in two minutes, wake him and send him down."

He had said it jokingly, in the hopes it might relieve the tension, but Marty frowned disapprovingly at him.

"No," she whispered. "Don't go."

"It's okay," he forced a smile. "And stop that. You're scaring me."

He eased down the stairs and as he reached the bottom, the elbow hitting wood sound came again. He turned the corner to find the front door open and that the wind had blown it up against the wall, making that noise.

They must not have closed it properly in all the confusion over the two pizzas.

He walked up to the door and closed it. He had to push it extra hard before he heard the click of it latching closed. Yes, he thought. That was it. It simply wasn't closed properly.

He turned the deadbolt, ensuring it was locked, and made his way down the hall and back up the stairs. At the top, he explained to Marty that it had only been the door, and it was then they both seemed to realize he had been wearing only his blue briefs and nothing else.

Marty looked up from glancing at his jockey shorts to find him looking back, suddenly embarrassed, but trying desperately to pretend he wasn't.

As he rounded the top of the stairs, he noticed Marty was back-lit from the light in her room. He could make out her naked silhouette and the sides of the large satiny globes of her bosom. He shyly averted his eyes, feeling an instant stirring in his groin and shuffled past her into his room, hoping she hadn't noticed.

"Goodnight," he said, thinking that if this were a movie he would have simply continued to eye her naked silhouette and she would notice the growing bulge in his shorts and they would embrace, collapsing onto the floor in her room and make frenzied love, fade to black and roll the credits.

But this wasn't a movie; it was real. And he was too hesitant, too unsure, and probably too excited over nothing.

"Goodnight, Carl," She crossed from her door and headed to the bathroom. "And," she paused taking another glance down at the bulge in his shorts, "thanks for the . . . uh . . . unspoken compliment."

"Uh," was all he managed to mutter as the door to the bathroom closed. He stood there a moment, alone with his semi-erection and feeling even more stupid.

Still unsure what to do and not wanting to look like an idiot, he went back into his room, leaving his door open, and crawled under the sheets.

As his mind was racing with thoughts of Marty and whether or not she might come into his room, and what might happen between the two of them if she did, he heard the noise of the imagined elbow hitting the wall.

The door had blown open again.

But how?

He had definitely locked it.

Marty's voice came from the bathroom, calling him.

He yelled back for her to stay in the bathroom and keep the door locked. Not that a locked door seemed to help, but he didn't know what else to suggest.

Another noise came from downstairs. Another sound of something colliding into a wall. And this time it was louder, closer; coming from the bottom of the stairs.

Rick called out groggily from his room for them to stop making all that noise and get the hell back to sleep.

That was when Carl heard the creaking groan of the step that was second from the top. The sound pierced the dark night the way that fingernails on a blackboard cut through a silent classroom.

"Rick!" Carl screamed. "There's someone in the house!" But he knew *someone* wasn't the right word; he should have said *something*.

As Carl watched, a dark shadow moved across the hall toward his bedroom door.

And with it came the smell of tomato sauce, cheese and pepperoni.

The young blond teenaged pizza guy was standing in Carl's doorway. His cheeks were even more sunken and emancipated than before, almost melting off his face like so much mozzarella. The waxy lips moved slowly, revealing a few moldy black teeth.

Carl realized he was saying something.

"Pissssssa," the tall thin figure slurred and as it went on to speak its top lip fell to the carpet. "Feffoni an mushoon."

It shifted another couple of steps into the room, reaching a thin, almost skeletal hand for Carl. As Carl watched, it continued to rapidly decompose in front of him.

Rick suddenly burst into the room with a wooden chair held over his head. He swung it down, breaking it across the intruder's back.

The blow sent the pizza guy forward onto Carl's bed, and he clambered along the bed, mouthing soundless words repeatedly. Carl bleakly wondered if its larynx had crumbled and fallen down its throat as he backed against the headboard of the bed.

Rick was lifting the chair again, looking at Carl, his eyes filled with questions. *What should I do?* His face seemed to be saying.

"He's already dead," Carl gasped. "You already tried once. We can't stop him like that."

A cold hand grasped Carl's bare foot, and Carl tried to thrash away from its cold moist touch.

What the hell was it trying to say?

"What?" Carl shrieked. "What the hell do you want from me?"

It pulled itself up Carl's legs and that was when Carl could see clearly into its eyes. He froze, and in the milky lens of its orbs he recognized something: fear.

It – no, not it; the teenager's name had been Steve -- Steve, was scared. Absolutely horrified. His eyes reminded Carl of something he'd seen in his own grandfather's eyes when he had been dying of cancer. It was a knowing, disturbed look that begged for the finality of death, the end of the pain.

"My God, Carl. It's all over you!" Rick yelled, and by that time Nancy and Marty were also at the bedroom door, standing behind Rick.

The creature, Steve, put a skeletal hand on Carl's shoulder and pulled himself up so that his face was level with Carl's. As his decayed lips moved, breaths of fetid air blew into Carl's face. The smell of rancid flesh churned his stomach.

But he could hear what Steve was trying to say.

"Th," Steve began. "Fh."

"Th. Fh."

Surf?

Nancy yelled out. "Do something, Rick!"

"Th. Tn. Fh."

"Like what? God, Carl. What can I do?"

"Th. Tn. Fh. Te."

Thirteen fifty? Thirteen fifty! Barely controlling the bile that rose in his throat, Carl asked: "Thirteen fifty?"

The flesh and bone head tilted and hope flooded through Steve's filmed eyes. For a brief second, Carl saw his own reflection in them. Steve's lips moved closer, quicker, more sure of the words.

"Thur. Tun. Fih. Tee." He repeatedly them frantically now.

"Rick! Get my wallet."

Rick fumbled with the junk on Carl's dresser, throwing a baseball cap off and discovering the black worn billfold beneath it. He grabbed it.

Carl stuck out his left hand and Rick placed the billfold in it. Steve repeated his relentless chant at a hurried pace, at times pressing his sour smelling facial flesh – what was left of it – against Carl's cheek.

Using one hand, Carl fingered open his wallet, found a bill and grasped it between two fingers, letting the wallet drop to the floor. He looked over at his hand. It was a green twenty-dollar bill.

"Thirteen fifty? Thirteen fifty?" Carl asked, screaming in a hysterical voice that cracked as he waved the bill in front of Steve's face. He let out a high-pitched cackle as he stuffed the bill into Steve's front shirt pocket. "Here you go. Keep the change!"

Steve's eyes remained on Carl and a smile that split his cheek open graced his face. He then stumbled off the bed and clambered out of the room.

They heard something bumping along the wall and tumbling down the stairs into the darkness below.

Moments later the front door slammed shut and the persistent scent of pizza was finally gone.

Behind the Screams

ONE OF THE things I still get plenty of comments from, both in reviews as well as in the emails sent to me from readers, is that they enjoy the "behind the story" notes that I add to my short stories.

And so, presented here are a few insights and some background information either on the inspiration or source for the story. If you're not a person who enjoys watching the special features on a DVD or the movie along with commentary from the actors or director, then I suggest you simply skip this last chapter. Thanks for reading a few of my stories. I hope you enjoyed them enough to want to read more of my fiction.

If, however, you do enjoy that "behind the curtains" peek into my fiction, then we still have a bit of time left on our walk together. Let me share with you some further background and insights into the tales you just read.

☠   ☠   ☠

About "Taste of Darkness"

I HAVE ALWAYS been fascinated by sensory deprivation tanks. I have never been in one (let's blame the mild claustrophobia, shall we?) but the concept of being in an environment where you can't see or hear anything strikes me as a little bit disconcerting.

As I considered the idea of one's senses seeming to disappear, I imagined a totally pure sensory deprivation environment, one where not just your sense of sight, sound, smell, touch and taste are muted, but they actually disappear, they flee from you. Wondering about that made me wonder where the senses might be going to when they disappear.

And that's where Mr. Jacks comes in.

Along with another concept that has long kicked around in the back of my mind. The concept of sanity and what sanity means has long interested me; likely starting from my enjoyment of reading *Hamlet* back in high school. As the young prince explores and questions his own sanity, I became intrigued with what sanity was and what insanity was as well.

I remember writing down in a notebook (the way I often jot down single lines or concepts that capture my attention) around the time I was enjoying *Hamlet* something like this:

"What if insanity isn't the lack of sane thought, but merely a side-effect of too much thought."

I enjoyed the "too much thought" concept.

Or, at least, the basic element of "too much." And that's where the idea of how Jacks might react to being over-loaded came to me.

This was long before the concept of mania or the up-swing of bipolar disorder/manic depression was well known or understood. And the concept, to me, might be that, in a manic state, in the over-active consumption of so much stimuli, perhaps *that* is one of the ways that insanity can strike. Like a battery that is over-loaded well beyond the normal charge it can hold.

And so, I wanted to explore that idea. With Mr. Jacks I wanted to explore ideas surrounding vicarious experiences and taking them to the extreme. And, though I wrote the original version of the story well before social media was as big as it is, the idea that it reflects upon a vicarious element is interesting.

I had to also push Dale into a state where he wasn't just willingly giving up his senses over to the darkness that allowed Jacks to consume them, but that he very forcefully thrust his senses out and into that darkness. That he committed a complete and unabashed sacrifice of himself for his daughter.

In the original version of the story, in his desire to save his daughter, Dale gives up his life, falls completely at prey to the darkness, losing not just the senses, but his very life and essence itself. But he knows his daughter will be fine; and he knows that Jacks is ultimately suffering. And while I did appreciate that concept, I wanted Dale to be able to know, for sure, that his Pumpkin was okay, that she was going to get out of it. So I switched the ending to give the reader more of a sense of that positive feeling.

And I did feel good about allowing Dale to come out a little scarred, and knowing the mistakes he had made which had led to the tragedy in the first place, but ensuring that it wasn't too late, that he could make the right decision and ensure his daughter was fine.

About "Little Things"

Originally published in Necrotic Tissue #13 *by Stygian Publications, 2011*

ONE NIGHT I was lying in bed and listening to an odd tapping sound that seemed to be coming from the ceiling. As I laid there, my eyes trying to focus in the darkness, I speculated about what might actually be causing that noise.

And then, what, to my wondering eyes did appear, but a tiny little bearded man without any reindeer.

Well, not at first. At first, all I could make out in the darkness was this tiny little pin-prick of a hole that slowly got larger. Then, after a few minutes of the insistent tapping, the hole was big enough for him to peek his tiny little dwarf head out.

At last, that's what my imagination conjured up as the odd tapping continued to echo through the dark.

And so, instead of letting the tapping that was preventing me from falling asleep from bothering me, I let the tapping amuse me as elements from this story gestated in my mind.

That's part of the special joy (and sometimes pain) of being a writer.

Even in an odd or strange or eerie moment, though you might be right there in it, part of your brain is also storing the event as potential fuel for another tale that you can craft and mold and share with others.

Once the little dwarf-like tiny creature appeared, I had no idea what his purpose was or why. So I wondered what might happen if only my main character, and not his wife, could perceive the little creature.

And, given that the creature, and the tiny little companions who eventually joined him, all had pick-axes, what else could they do but mine the very first person they physically encountered when they arrived.

Even as I was writing the tale, I wasn't sure if they were there to torture Joy or Daniel. Since Joy was completely oblivious to the way they were mining her flesh, they must have been there to haunt and mock Daniel.

One editor that I sent this story to mused that his thought the little mining dwarves were allegorical for a cancer that was eating away at her flesh. That was an interesting perspective.

I realized, only as I got to the end of the tale, how it was going to end.

Because, to be completely honest, as I was crafting the story, the only thing I knew was that the little men, the havoc they were wreaking on Joy's body, were going to cause a rift between the two of them; one in which Daniel questions his sanity. And, unable to watch these little creatures destroy the woman he loves, Daniel feels obligated to explain what caused the marriage to dissolve and comes up with the pun-inspired line of not being able to live with the little things.

Looking back on the story, I wonder if there's more to it than just a cute little pun. I wonder if the little men represent what can happen in almost any relationship when one person in that relationship focuses on the little things rather than the larger picture, or the entire person.

That one small thing that bothers you; that tiny little element that perhaps nobody else can see can eat away at you, become your entire focus so that you no longer see the other person, you just see the flaws, those tiny little flaws that you just can't live without.

I realized that those little men might be real or they might not be real. They might exist or they might be representative of Daniel starting to focus on all those little flaws that a person usually brushes aside.

They might actually just be an allegory for the decay that can happen in a relationship when the focus is skewed in such a direction.

In any case, it's a story I enjoy.

And sometimes, when I'm lying in bed and staring at the ceiling in the middle of the night, pondering about what it is that woke me, I wonder if I'll ever hear that tap tap tapping.

About "The Pizza Man"

Originally published in EerieCon Chapbook #14 *by The Buffalo Fantasy League, 2014*

THE VERY FIRST version of this story was written late one evening in 1988 while I was in first year university and me and my house-mates were perturbed by two unsolicited pizza deliveries on the same night.

It was either a strange mistake (since we had just moved in the previous week), or a practical joke of sorts – but the part of my mind that finds dark and more disturbing ways to explain situations came up with the murdered teenager concept.

So I went up to my room, turning on my Commodore 64 and started cranking out the story on my word processor. When I finished it several hours later, I printed it on my 12-pin dot matrix printer and read it to Maureen (who became Marty) and Nana (who became Nancy), two of my roommates, who quite enjoyed the tale; particularly the fact that it was set in our house and featured all of us. My cousin Rodney, who was the inspiration for Rick, shrugged it off, the same way Rick shrugged things off in the story.

It was a cute short tale, but there wasn't much to it other than a dead guy who kept showing up at the door and a bug-infested barfing gross-out scene.

But I kept picking away at the story over the years, working on turning the characters from caricatures and into developed people, (Modifying their names from our names and into the characters they would become) noodling with the plot, and coming up with the story.

I couldn't decide whether I'd call the story "The Pizza Man" in the hokey horror comic book style of story it was meant to be, or call it "Thirteen-Fifty" since paying the pizza guy what he was coming to collect is the key element that Carl uses to finally release poor Steve from his purgatorial existence.

I ended up sending this story out to a few beta readers to help me fix it up and determine the actual title – and that's how I landed on the title I used. I also realized that perhaps calling it "Thirteen-Fifty" might be too much of a hint towards the solution that Carl comes up with, even though I'm still a bit partial to that because it provides the answer right there in the title.

Another thing that I kept going back and forth on in the re-writes for this story were making Steve, the pizza guy, a ghost VS a "walking dead" character. Because he, ultimately, is a combination of both. When writing a horror story, it's still important for me for the story to contain a consistent internal logic. And it's still something I struggle with when thinking about this one. Steve, the ghostly figure, will continue to return to the house, running through the "movie-reel" last moments of his life, trapped in the purgatory of the last few minutes of his life. Carl's act of helping him to "complete" his last delivery mission allows him to finally be at rest.

But, to heighten the horror of the situation, it made more sense to play off of the rotting and decomposing nature of his state. For the gross-out moments with the pizza the kids eat, for the physicality of the dead body crawling across Carl's bed and grasping at him, breathing fetid breaths at him in desperation. I wanted Carl, and the reader, to be both mortified, but also to feel compassion for this poor trapped soul. Therefore, combining the ghost and undead elements seemed to be the only way to pull that off.

Back to a few elements from the story that were important for me to attempt to express. First, Carl, like me, was from a small town, moving to what, to him, was a large city. A new town, a new experience (University), and all the uneasiness that comes with that – in particular, the fact I had never lived away from home – were all a recipe for tension, unease and nervousness. Combine that with (like me), an over-active imagination and a fear of the unknown, and you have the perfect toppings (yes, that's a pizza pun) for a scary story.

One of the things that wouldn't leave my mind when I had moved into my bedroom in this house in a different city was the thought of all the other people who might have lived in that space, slept in that same bedroom over the years. It's a thought that still fascinates me today, considering, especially, the hundreds of different hotel rooms in cities all over the world that I've slept in over the past half dozen years alone.

For example, when the light bulb in my bedroom burned out in my first week there, I spent an inordinate amount of time speculating about when it was last changed, who last changed it, and the circumstances surrounding that occurrence. It was a small thing, but one of hundreds of little things that might have happened in that house, in that space in all the years before I had arrived. But that led, of course, to the wonder about what bad things, what evil things, might have taken place in the house before we arrived. Such as a previous tenant doing bad things to people. Like abducting, torturing and murdering poor Steve.

Do you ever wonder the same thing, in particular when you're staying in a hotel room that likely had thousands of others sleeping there before? Do you ever wonder about the thousands of unique situations, the interesting stories, the conversations, the happy, sad, angry, confusing, fearful moments that might have occurred there? For me, that's one of the countless ways that inspiration for stories come to me. And if that's something you never thought about, I hope that it's more of a point of interest for you to reflect on and not something that causes you to lose sleep in the middle of the night.

Particularly not when you wake in the middle of the night and either hear or smell something that seems a little bit out of place.

Conclusion: One Last Whispering Cry

THANK YOU FOR following me along, not just in reading the stories, but in reading these stories behind the stories. I hope that you enjoyed the experience of both.

Short stories are where I first cut my teeth on writing, and they will always hold a special place in my heart. You can explore so much in such a short number of words; and, in particular when it comes to the horror genre, you can craft something that doesn't necessarily have to have a happy ending; and that can lead to a bit more suspense in the reader.

Okay, sure, two of the stories have "happy" endings. But one of them does end on a bit of a sad or bitter note. As Meatloaf sang, two out of three ain't bad.

If you enjoyed this little collection, I'd greatly appreciate if you took the time to leave a review for it. It might seem like a little thing, but the one or two minutes it takes goes a long way towards helping a writer find new readers. And if you're so inclined to send me a note to let me know what you thought, that's cool too. My email is mark@markleslie.ca.

(You can also sign up for my newsletter at **www.markleslie.ca** to stay informed of my new releases and get a full-sized eBook for free)

If you weren't satisfied with what you read, I'm happy to get an email from you just the same. Your experience and thoughts are just as important. I'm always looking to grow as a writer, and learning why a story didn't work for a reader can be an important part of that process.

But in any case, thanks for accompanying me; thanks for listening to some of those nocturnal screams along with me. And perhaps we'll encounter each other between the digital pages of another book some-day. Do please tip your hat and say hi so that I don't mistake you for one of those scary monsters that I believe sometimes stalk me from the shadows.

-   *Mark Leslie, April*
    2020

About the Author

Mark Leslie is a writer, editor, and bookseller who was born and grew up in Sudbury, Ontario, spent many years in Ottawa, Ontario and currently lives in Southern Ontario. Claiming that he has always been frightened of the monster under his bed, Mark loves crafting eerie and creepy tales that follow the "what if" questions that occur to him every time he takes a peek into the shadows. And he spends a lot of times looking at the shadows and listening for the screams. You can learn more about Mark and sign up for his author newsletter at **www.markleslie.ca**.

Selected Other Books by Mark Leslie

Novels

A Canadian Werewolf in New York
Evasion
I, Death

Short Story Collections

One Hand Screaming
Active Reader
Nobody's Hero

Anthologies (as Editor)

Campus Chills
Tesseracts Sixteen: Parnassus Unbound
Fiction River: Editor's Choice
Fiction River: Feel the Fear
Fiction River: Feel the Love
Fiction River: Superstitious

Non-Fiction / Paranormal / Ghost Stories

Haunted Hamilton
Spooky Sudbury
Tomes of Terror
Creepy Capital
Haunted Hospitals
Macabre Montreal

The NOCTURNAL SCREAMS Series

 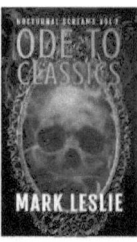